This book belongs
to

Jeffrey Fauci

children's
choice

ROUND
ROBIN

JACK KENT

Prentice-Hall, Inc. – Englewood Cliffs, N.J.

 A Children's Choice® Book Club Edition From Scholastic Book Services

To my Junie

ISBN 0-590-75934-5
Printed in the United States of America

At first the little robin was like
any other baby bird. Most of him was
head and the rest of him was hungry.

He ate,

and he ate,

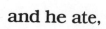

and he ate,

and he ate,

until he looked more like a ball
than a bird.

Everybody called him Round Robin.

The other birds fluttered about
from tree to tree.
"Come fly with us, Round Robin," they said.

But Round Robin was too fat to fly.

When he wanted to go anywhere, he hopped.

Hippety, hoppety, boppety, BUMP.

With sometimes more bumps than hops.

But mostly he just stayed where he was.

All he wanted to do was eat.

When fall came, the robins began
to fly south.

"Come along, Round Robin," they said.
"Soon snow will cover the ground,
 and food will be hard to find."

So Round Robin headed south, too.
Hippety, hoppety, boppety, BUMP.

It was slow going.

All that hopping made him hungry.
So every few minutes he stopped to eat.
This slowed him down even more.

Round Robin had not gone very far
when winter caught up with him.

Hopping in the snow was hard work.

It was easier on the road, where
automobiles had packed the snow
as hard as ice.

Hippety, hoppety, slippety, SLIDE.

But it was dangerous.

"If you don't want to get run over,"
warned a field mouse, "stick to
the byways."

So Round Robin did.

The snow kept getting deeper and deeper.
But Round Robin struggled on.

"I'm starving!" he complained one day.
"There's nothing at all to *eat!*"

"Oh, I wouldn't say that!" said a fox,
who suddenly appeared from behind a tree.
"*You* look very tasty to *me!*"

He licked his lips and leaped at Round Robin.

Everything happened so fast that Round Robin
didn't have time to think. He was even
more surprised than the fox when he found
himself *flying.*

He wasn't round anymore.

"It's from all that exercise and nothing
to eat," said Round Robin as he flew south.

He flew

and he flew

and he flew.

And he didn't dare stop
until he caught up with
the rest of the robins.

It was warm and sunny in the South.
With no snow on the ground, food was
easy to find. And Round Robin was
oh, so hungry!

So he ate,

and he ate,

and he ate,

and he ate,

until he looked more like a ball
than a bird.

It had taken Round Robin all winter to make the trip. Now it was spring and the robins were beginning to fly north again.

"Come along, Round Robin," they said.

"It's time to go home."

So Round Robin sighed a deep sigh
and started on the trip back north.
Hippety, hoppety, boppety, BUMP.